Talking with Artists

Talking with Artists

Conversations with

Victoria Chess · Pat Cummings
Leo and Diane Dillon · Richard Egielski
Lois Ehlert · Lisa Campbell Ernst · Tom Feelings
Steven Kellogg · Jerry Pinkney · Amy Schwartz
Lane Smith · Chris Van Allsburg
and David Wiesner

compiled and edited by Pat Cummings

BRADBURY PRESS ▲ NEW YORK

Maxwell Macmillan Canada   Toronto
Maxwell Macmillan International
New York   Oxford   Singapore   Sydney

Bradbury Press
Macmillan Publishing Company
866 Third Avenue
New York, NY 10022

Maxwell Macmillan Canada, Inc.
1200 Eglinton Avenue East
Suite 200
Don Mills, Ontario M3C 3N1

Macmillan Publishing Company is part of the
Maxwell Communication Group of Companies.

First edition
Printed and bound in the United States of America
10 9 8 7 6 5 4 3 2 1
Typography by Julie Y. Quan
Book production by Daniel Adlerman

LIBRARY OF CONGRESS CATALOGING-IN-PUBLICATION DATA

Talking with artists : Conversations with Victoria Chess, Pat Cummings, Leo and Diane Dillon, Richard Egielski, Lois Ehlert, Lisa Campbell Ernst, Tom Feelings, Steven Kellogg, Jerry Pinkney, Amy Schwartz, Lane Smith, Chris Van Allsburg, and David Wiesner / compiled and edited by Pat Cummings.—1st ed.
p.   cm.
Includes bibliographical references.
Summary: Fourteen distinguished picture book artists talk about their early art experiences, answer questions most frequently asked by children, and offer encouragement to those who would like to become artists.
ISBN 0–02–724245–5
1. Illustrators—United States—Biography—Juvenile literature.
[1. Illustrators. 2. Artists.] I. Cummings, Pat.
NC975.T34 1992
741.6′42′092273—dc20
[B]   91-9982

For Barbara Lalicki

CONTENTS

ear Reader,

A few years ago, I got a letter from a girl in Connecticut. I had just visited her school. A lot of the people in this book go out to schools and libraries to talk to people about what we all do: illustrate books.

But, anyway, this girl said that she loved to draw. She added that she had wanted to be an illustrator when she grew up—that is, until I came to her school. Then she explained that it seemed too hard and she was just going to be a lawyer instead!

I think becoming a lawyer must be pretty hard. I always thought making pictures was fun. If you really love doing something, it doesn't seem like work at all. So even though art can be your *job*, it still can be very enjoyable. Maybe lawyers think law is fun, too.

Most of the artists in this book have always loved to draw. They were probably the "class artists" when they were younger. Do you have someone in your class who can really draw dinosaurs, or unicorns, or cars? Maybe *you're* the "class artist." Maybe you already have a specialty—something that you draw better than anyone else.

Well, there are a lot of different kinds of illustration jobs. If you notice, there are illustrations in magazines, on movie posters, in newspapers, on the sides of buses, and even on the back of your box of cereal in the morning! And somebody, somewhere, was asked to draw each picture and got paid for doing it.

The fourteen artists in this book will tell you fourteen different stories about how and why they became illustrators. Some of them have done a lot of different kinds of illustrations. All of them are illustrating children's books now, and you have probably read some of their books. They have also answered some of the questions that we're asked most frequently when we visit schools. You'll see a piece of artwork from when they were kids and a sample of the artwork they do now.

I hope that if you like drawing, or, better still, if you LOVE it, that you will stick with it. You might do comic books one day, or draw cars or clothes or book covers. But don't be afraid of the "work" in "artwork." Keep drawing. That's all we did. We just kept drawing.

—Pat Cummings

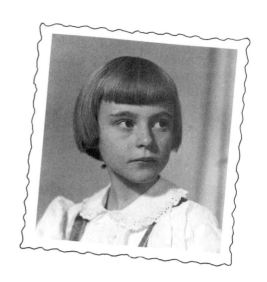

Victoria Chess

MY STORY

Birthday: November 16, 1939

I was born in Chicago, Illinois, in 1939 and brought up in the small New England town of Washington, Connecticut. I now live not very far from there. I spent a whole year living in France when I was seven. Luckily, thanks to a Swiss nanny I had as a child, I spoke French even before I moved there. In fact, I was three years old before I could speak English—and four years old before I would admit it. It's interesting what people say around you when they think you don't understand!

I lived for a total of fifteen years in Manhattan and made occasional forays into odd corners of the world. For example, I once lived in Beirut for three years. I was doing artwork even then, sometimes working for the United Nations Relief Work Agency. Some of the countries I got to visit were Jordan, Syria, Iraq, and Turkey.

I don't miss living in the city now. I have a river that runs at the bottom of my yard. For that matter, I have a yard. Also, there are plenty of other illustrators living nearby, and they are readily available for shoptalk about the kind of work we all do. We might listen to each other's complaints or offer congratulations.

All children draw, but I think illustrators are the ones who keep doing it after fifth grade. I used to draw horses. Thousands and thousands of horses. In fact, I learned to draw other things by simply adding antlers to make the horses into stags, or putting trees, castles, witches, and princesses into the background. I would easily spend hours poring over a book called _How to Draw Animals_. I remember drawing and redrawing, trying to get my pictures right.

I really adored the fairy tales written by the Brothers Grimm and also the stories of the nineteenth century by the Comtesse de Segur. My favorite was "Bluebeard" by Charles Perrault.

I was very impressed with the art that went with the stories. In many of them, the pictures were made with steel engravings, I think. That is a technique in which an artist must scratch the drawing onto a steel plate in order to print a picture from it. I remember that the story illustrations were gloomy, threatening, and to me, very exciting. That took care of the serious side of things. For fun, I thought that nothing could top the Krazy Kat and Pogo comics.

I attended the Mary C. Wheeler School for Girls in Providence, Rhode Island. Most of my time there was spent drawing, reading unassigned books, and avoiding Latin studies, math, and the sciences. Consequently, I was asked to leave. I then went to school at La Chatelainie in St. Blaise, Switzerland. More girls. We had to ski for four hours a day—and I can't stand heights or speed! So I got to be very good not only at French but at "Sneaking Out."

After that, there were a few years spent at the School of the Museum of Fine Arts in Boston, Massachusetts—where, because of a rich, enjoyable social life and incomplete assignments, I was also asked to leave.

I got to illustrate my first book almost by accident and discovered there is nothing like the promise of money to develop good work habits.

Twenty-five years later, I still get up every morning happy and eager to get on with whatever assignment I have at the moment. It seems to me that so many people have only the recreational times in their lives to look forward to. It is such a blessing not to be among them. In the end, I work to please myself. I only hope that children will enjoy my pictures, and learn to laugh at the world and not take themselves too seriously.

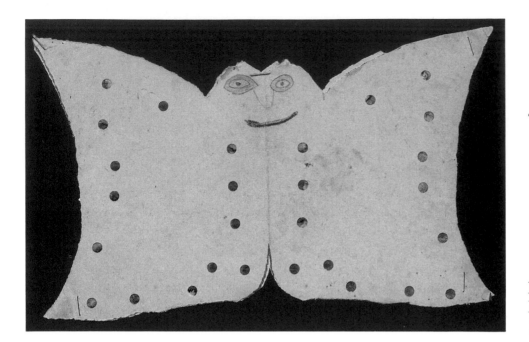

Butterfly. Age 6.
Paper and pencil,
11½ × 7½".

1. Where do you get your ideas from?

I really get my ideas from all of the things that I see. I travel a lot and always like to take many photographs on my trips. I also have books with pictures of houses and furniture, animals and trees, all kinds of things, so that if I don't know what something looks like I can look it up.

2. What is a normal day like for you?

A normal day for me is to wake up at five-thirty in the morning and have some coffee first (there's a pot I keep right by the bed). I like to stare out of the window and watch the sky as it changes. Then, I get up at around seven, fix myself some breakfast, mess around the house a bit, and start to work at eight, when my husband leaves for his office. I work until two and then I go and do something else.

3. Where do you work?

I work in my studio, which was converted from what used to be the garage. It has a lot of windows, four tables, and a chair that is hanging from the ceiling. Also, on the *inside* of my studio, I have a lime tree, a lemon tree, two orange trees, and a huge vine that is growing all over the place. When you live in the country, you can have trees indoors!

4. Do you have any children? Any pets?

Yes, I do. I have one son, Sam Dickerson, who's all grown up now. He's away in college in Scotland. He seems to love to travel as much as I do.

I've got one enormous, hairy dog named Bruno and a smaller, fat one who looks just like a pig. Her name is Claire. I also have three cats: Mrs. Bloom, who is black and very boring; Zazou, who is orange and very exciting; and Pearl, who is part Siamese, kind of cream colored, and looks like she's wearing sneakers. Pearl is quite a hunter—she's a rat-killer!

5. What do you enjoy drawing the most?

What I enjoy drawing most are lizards, but I haven't yet done a book about them. I'm not sure just what it is about them that I like so much.

6. Do you ever put people you know in your pictures?

I always put people I know in my pictures, whether I mean to or not. They just seem to appear.

7. What do you use to make your pictures?

I prefer to use liquid watercolors, paintbrushes, and colored pencils. I use technical pens, as well. These are pens with metal points that can make lines that are always the same width. If you push too hard on your pen, the line won't suddenly get wider like a felt-tip pen line might.

I also use technical inks—inks that will not run if you get them wet, so you can paint right over them. Because they are waterproof, they won't mix in with the next color you're using once they have dried.

Calendar Cat, 1990

For example, if you look closely at my picture from *A Hippopoto-musn't*, you can see that there are little white dots on the green plant in the window. If I had painted a white dot over regular green ink, the dot would have turned light green when the colors started to blend. Using the technical inks, I could count on the white staying white.

8. How did you get to do your first book?

I had been doing illustrations for different kinds of trade magazines and had always wanted to do a picture book. I remember going out once with my portfolio to show samples of my artwork to a publisher. After looking over my portfolio, the editor I had shown it to told me that she thought I was "deranged." I think I must have shown her some of my lizard drawings.

I had a friend who was a literary agent, a person who will take your work to publishers and try to sell it. As it happened, this agent also represented an author who had written a funny story that needed illustrations. This author was pretty famous, and his publisher was willing to let him pick any artist that he wanted to work with. Usually the publisher decides who will illustrate a book.

The agent showed my drawings to the author and, luckily, he liked my work and thought it was right for his book. I had finished all of the pictures for the book before the publisher even got a chance to see them!

I got to do my first book because I knew someone important who could help me. And one book led to another and another. I can't ever pay that person back, but I do try to help young artists get started.

2. What is a normal day like for you?

I don't have any normal days because every job is different. Some days I meet with my editor, some days I get up early and work all day. Sometimes I work all night. Some days I teach a class at a local college. And sometimes I'm traveling to schools and libraries around the country. I work just about every day, and I work most of the time I'm home. If I have a deadline I am trying to meet, I might not leave the house for days at a time. I'll work until I'm sleepy, sleep until I wake up, and start again. Usually, I do try to go to the gym, and I might go to the movies to reward myself for finishing a page. There are usually thirty-two pages in a book. That can get to be a lot of movies.

3. Where do you work?

I live and work in a big loft in beautiful downtown Brooklyn, New York. If I look out of my back windows, I see the Statue of Liberty. Looking out of the window near my desk, I see the Brooklyn Bridge. It's great on the Fourth of July! There are fifteen windows and five skylights, so there's plenty of sunlight and, sometimes, moonlight.

My drawing table, desk, shelves, and filing cabinets are on one side of the loft, and my husband's work area is right across from mine. The whole place is one big, open space that we are always working on.

4. Do you have any children? Any pets?

We don't have any children, but we have talked about trying to find a twelve-year-old who likes to do dishes.

We have a cat named Cash who is very smart. She is on the cover of *Storm in the Night.* She comes when she's called, sits if you tell her to, and fetches if you throw her toy. I think she might be a dog.

5. What do you enjoy drawing the most?

People I know and faces in general. There is so much going on in a person's face. I like fantasy, too . . . drawing things that only exist in the imagination.

6. **Do you ever put people you know in your pictures?**

Definitely. Sometimes I do it to surprise the person. I might use old family photos or take new ones to use as reference. I draw my husband, Chuku, a lot. He's just about the only one who will pose for me at two-thirty in the morning. I've drawn neighbors, neighbors' pets, and friends who might even ask me to change their hairstyles or make them look thinner. I will also find models to draw who fit the image I have in my mind of the characters in the book.

I used my sister Linda and my niece Keija on the cover of *Just Us Women*. Keija told me once that her picture was the only reason people read the book! That book is filled with family: my mother, Chuku, my brother-in-law Hassan, my grandfather, my sister Barbara, and a friend or two. It makes the book more personal for me.

7. **What do you use to make your pictures?**

Everything. I like to use different materials. Sometimes it's big fun, but sometimes it's disastrous. I use watercolors and colored pencils most often; gouache, acrylics, pastels, airbrush, and pen and ink sometimes. I've experimented with collage and even rubber stamps, but I don't think I've tried half of the stuff I see in the art supply stores.

I also maintain a big picture file for reference. If I have to draw an armadillo, it helps a lot to have a picture to look at while I work.

8. **How did you get to do your first book?**

I put some illustrations from art school into a portfolio and went to see editors at publishing houses. They gave me good advice but no work. Then an editor saw my artwork in a newsletter and offered me a book to illustrate. I was so excited that when she asked if I knew what to do, I said, "Sure, no problem." I didn't have a clue how to start, but I didn't want to let her know.

I knew somebody, who knew somebody, who knew someone who used to know Tom Feelings, a children's book illustrator whose work I admired. So I looked in the phone book, called Tom up, and asked him if he would help me. He was wonderful. He gave me advice on how to pick which parts of the story to illustrate and how to decide where the pages should turn. He reminded me always to leave lots of room for the

C.L.O.U.D.S. 1986.
Airbrush, watercolor, and pencil, 15½ × 10".
Published by Lothrop, Lee & Shepard Books.

words to fit, to be sure that the character looks like the same person all the way through the book, and to try and keep important details away from the middle of the book, where the pages are sewn together. You don't want your reader pulling the book apart to see something important that's been hidden in the seam!

Tom taught me a lot that afternoon. He and many other illustrators still inspire me. I still learn from looking at their work. The most important thing I learned from Tom that day was that we have to help each other. He helped me get started, and I never forget that when someone who wants to illustrate calls me.

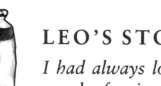

Leo Dillon
Diane Dillon

LEO'S STORY

Leo's Birthday: March 2, 1933

I had always loved to draw. I was forever scrawling something— people, furniture, animals, drums, horns, and flags.

My parents did not pay too much attention, since it was taken for granted that that was what Leo did. Draw pictures.

My father was involved in the Garvey movement. Marcus Garvey was a great political figure of the 1930s. Ralph Volman, a friend of my father's, was also dedicated to this cause. He would come to our house every week where, along with others, they would hold discussions and plan demonstrations.

Mr. Volman was a painter, a poet, and a musician. He always talked to me about art. He would show me his beautiful pen-and-ink drawings, read me some of his poetry, and bring me books about painting. He

"Make life an art!"
—Leo Dillon

Desert with Mountains. Age 9. Watercolor, 12 × 9".

We choose what materials we will use depending on the look we feel is right for the story. If we need something light and airy we might use pastel or pencil. For something more painterly, we might choose acrylics.

8. How did you get to do your first book?

After graduating from art school we started illustrating album covers and book covers. One of our young adult book jackets had a Native American theme. An editor who saw it happened to have a manuscript that she needed illustrated. She thought our style would be great for her story. She asked us if we'd be interested in doing a book and we said "yes." We've been doing picture books ever since.

We like to explore our own subplots. In *Why Mosquitoes Buzz in People's Ears*, we put a little red bird in every scene who witnesses everything as the story unfolds. He wasn't really part of the story, but we liked making his role more important with every turn of the page.

The Tale of the Mandarin Ducks by Katherine Paterson. 1990.

Watercolor and pastel, 15 × 10¼″. Published by Lodestar.

Richard Egielski

MY STORY

Birthday: July 16, 1952

My love for making pictures began when I was very young. So young that I can't remember how old I was when I started drawing.

I do remember that television had something to do with it. I loved the Jon Gnagy show. It featured a goateed man in a plaid shirt. He would begin a drawing with rectangles, ovals, and cubes and then transform them into portraits, landscapes, and still lifes.

One Christmas my parents gave me a Jon Gnagy kit. It contained paper, pencils, charcoal, a kneaded eraser, a pencil sharpener and an instruction book. I spent many a happy Saturday morning drawing along with the show.

Also, I had a Venus Paradise colored-pencil set and a bunch of factory-reject, blank, lineless copybooks that became my first sketchbooks. These I filled with drawings, based on movies, of King Kong, Frankenstein, dinosaurs, medieval knights, Roman soldiers battling Hercules, ships, planes, and flying saucers.

I made things up a lot. I really liked watching "Betty Boop" and "Popeye" on television, and after the show would go off, I would draw cartoons of them in all kinds of situations. I copied cartoon characters from the comics in the newspaper, too, which was really good drawing practice for me. I watched a lot of movies. In fact, I liked drawing in sequences, wanting to show one scene happening after another, just like in the movies.

But drawing was something that I did for my own entertainment, just for fun. The possibility that it might lead to a career didn't occur to me.

For years I had been going to a horrible Catholic school where the students were routinely beaten by the nuns who taught there. I hated going to that school.

However, in the eighth grade we students had to decide what high schools we would apply to. Because of my experience in grammar school, the idea of attending a Catholic high school filled me with terror. My parents would not allow me to go to the local public high school. They said that the standards were not high enough. Luckily for me, the New York City public school system had distributed a booklet containing descriptions and requirements of the specialized high schools. Here were public schools with standards acceptable to my parents. Among the schools listed was the High School of Art and Design. Along with the required academic subjects like English, math, and science, the students took art classes that would supply them with the skills necessary to pursue a career in commercial art. It sounded great to me. I took the test and I presented a portfolio full of my best drawings. I was accepted. I was ecstatic.

And it was great. There was a wonderfully free and progressive atmosphere at Art and Design. With the help of many terrific teachers in both the academics and the arts, I grew as a person as well as an artist.

One of my art teachers there was Irwin Greenberg, who had taught John Steptoe when he attended Art and Design. John was something of a legend and an inspiration because he had left school at seventeen and, at that young age, had illustrated *Stevie*, his first children's book.

After graduating from the High School of Art and Design, I went on to study at Pratt Institute and Parsons School of Design. At different times I've been a painter and a magazine illustrator and done advertising and graphic design as well. I took a course in book illustration, and I've been doing children's books ever since.

"Just draw!"
—Richard Egielski

Battle Scene. Age 15.
Oil painting, 20 × 16″.

1. Where do you get your ideas from?

The text contains all the raw material that I need to design my pictures. I particularly like stories that do not contain a lot of physical description of characters or places. It is much more interesting to develop characters based on their actions and personalities.

I might use pieces of things from my own life, but real life never seems to fit exactly into the story I am working on. So mostly I use my imagination and I *invent*. One interesting example of inventing occurred when I illustrated a story by Arthur Yorinks called *It Happened in Pinsk*. Arthur and I knew that there was a real city named Minsk but didn't know that there was a Pinsk. So I made up the town setting based on scenes from a lot of different European and Eastern European cities. I used images of every place from Venice to Moscow, and freely invented settings. I drew Pinsk, its buildings, and its street scenes the way I imagined they might have looked.

One day Arthur got a letter from an elderly couple who had just happened to find our book in a bookstore while they were driving around. The letter said that they had both been born and raised in Pinsk and looking at the pictures had reminded them so much of their hometown that they just had to write. It was all just as they remembered it! It was quite a surprise to find out that Pinsk was an actual place. It was even more amazing to find that my drawings had somehow turned out to be realistic.

2. What is a normal day like for you?

There is no such thing as a normal day for me. Some days the pictures come easily and some days they don't come at all. Some days I get to the drawing table early and some days I sleep late and work well into the evening.

I do have to take a few breaks, though, because every three hours or so my dog comes in and gets me. At first she will just sit and watch me. Then she starts crawling closer and closer, inching up on me. Finally she gets so impatient that she paws me until it's clear that I have to stop working. I take a break and go outside and throw a Frisbee around with her for a while. That usually holds her for about another three hours.

3. Where do you work?

My studio is in the attic. I work at one end and my wife, Denise Saldutti, who is also a children's book illustrator, works at the other end. It is a long room with two skylights and one window at either end. Denise's window overlooks the backyard and the Delaware River, and mine overlooks the street.

I like to listen to the radio while I am working. I like to listen to informational programs and all kinds of music, from rock and roll to classical to jazz, flipping from one station to another if I get bored.

4. Do you have any children? Any pets?

Yes, a brand-new baby boy named Ian. We also have the dog that I mentioned before. Her name is Daisy. She makes frequent appearances in our books.

5. What do you enjoy drawing the most?

If the story excites me, I like drawing just about anything. I particularly like drawing people—especially one person set in an interior.

6. Do you ever put people you know in your pictures?

Yes, but it is more or less unintentional. Sometimes, when I'm making up a character, I'll think to myself, "This sort of looks like so and so." And I'll go with that and draw them as I remember them. It just happens.

In *Oh, Brother* one of the characters was a somewhat balding butler. As I was working, the character started to look a lot like my editor. He didn't mind showing up in the book, but he said he really would have preferred being a prince or a king. A lot of people also tell me that the main character in *It Happened in Pinsk* looks like Maurice Sendak.

I occasionally stick my wife in pictures, in the background in the crowd, though. If she were close up I would have to put in details and make it really look like her. I think the pressure might be too much!

7. What do you use to make your pictures?

To date, all of my pictures are watercolors on various paper surfaces. I choose different paper for different books, and I alter my technique by what I feel the story requires.

I have a lot of fine arts books around to look at and a collection of picture books as well. I have a file of pictures that I thought would be helpful to look at when I needed reference material, but I find that I don't really use it much after all.

8. How did you get to do your first book?

It took years for me to get my first picture book. In the beginning, many editors said that my pictures were too weird for children's picture books.

I had taken a course on illustrating books that was being taught by Maurice Sendak at Parsons. I had never really thought of doing children's books before that. I had been rounded up with some other students when they decided to offer the course and asked to join the class. It was in this class that I first realized that children's books were the perfect place to do the sequential drawings that I liked to do.

One day, by chance, I met Arthur Yorinks, an author, in the school elevator, of all places. It turned out that he was searching for just the right illustrator for his stories. He liked my pictures; I liked his stories.

I made a dummy of his story *Sid and Sol* and we sold it to a publisher. We've been working together ever since. Since then, Arthur and I have teamed up to do *Louis the Fish*, *Hey, Al*, and *Oh, Brother*, among other books.

Oh, Brother by Arthur Yorinks. 1989.
Watercolor, 11 × 18". Published by Farrar, Straus & Giroux.

MY STORY

Birthday: November 9, 1934

When I was growing up in Beaver Dam, Wisconsin, my family lived in the small house where my mother still lives. Everyone in my house seemed to be making something. I was the oldest of three children, and I was expected to set a good example for my younger brother and sister. We were expected to entertain ourselves and clean up our messes. Both my mother and dad had hobbies. My mother liked to sew and made most of my clothes. She saved fabric scraps for me and taught me to sew when I was eight years old. My dad worked in a dairy and spent his spare time in his basement workshop, smoking a cigar and building things, most times of wood. It didn't take me long to learn to beg for scraps of wood and nails.

I always had a ready supply of art materials, but not necessarily traditional ones like paper and paint. In fact, colored construction paper was pale next to my cloth scraps. To this day I sometimes prefer to paint my own papers to get just the right color or texture.

My mother's sewing machine was in a room most families would have called the dining room, but we had a piano, so we called it the music room. Next to the piano was a corner space just big enough for a card table. I was allowed to leave my current projects spread out there to return to when I had free time. I'm sure there were times when my mother or dad would have loved to dump the whole mess into the garbage, but they never did. (My brother recently reminded me of one of my dad's sayings: "A place for everything, everything in its place.")

I spent so many happy hours at that table, and I considered it my "turf." Having this place to work was special to me.

I did a lot of painting and drawing at that table, but I never felt as comfortable with drawing as I did with making things.

When I drew I needed a big eraser. I never knew whether the mouth on a drawing would look better one inch closer to the nose unless I did the drawing over and over again. But if I cut out a mouth of paper, I could move it around until it fit in just the right spot and then I could glue it down.

Beaver Dam was a small town. I never knew any artists personally as I was growing up, but somehow I knew that I wanted to be one. So, at that same card table during my senior year, I painted some samples of my artwork and filled out a scholarship application for Layton School of Art. I was overjoyed to get a letter of acceptance and a scholarship. I left late that summer for Milwaukee (about seventy miles from home) and, naturally, I took the card table with me.

I got a job after school running a switchboard and I worked until nine most evenings. I loved going to art school. Most of the students enjoyed the same things I did. The best part of the day for me was going to my room after work to solve the art assignments. I would sit at the card table, now made into a drawing board by leaning a bread board on a can, and do my art projects. By the time I graduated four years later, the card table was splattered with paint and ink. My dad made a new top for it out of plywood.

Now, you may not believe it, but I still have that card table, folded up in the closet next to my studio, although my dad died about ten years ago. The wooden top he made now has some holes drilled right through it (an accident during a framing project), lots of scratches from cutting material with sharp scissors (now I'm sewing my own clothes), and some razor-blade scars from cutting mats for my illustrations. I wonder if I would have grown up to be an artist without that card table? All I know is that I'm still cutting and pasting and still enjoying life as an artist.

"If you're interested in being creative, have a little spot in your house where you can leave your things so that when you do want to do something you're ready."

—Lois Ehlert

Potholder. Age 8.
Stitched fabric, 6½ × 9".

1. Where do you get your ideas from?

It is sometimes difficult to know just where ideas come from. Creativity is part of a person's makeup, I think. It's something I feel very lucky about. I've worked hard to develop this gift but I still think I was born with certain ideas and feelings waiting to burst out!

I realize I write and draw things I know and care about. For instance, having a garden most of my life and loving color gave me ideas for a book. My writing usually goes hand in hand with my art. If I illustrate other writers' books, I try to show their feelings, too.

2. What is a normal day like for you?

I work most days. Most people think since I work for myself I work only when I feel like it. Too bad it's not true for me. I usually start about 8:00 A.M. and go all day. I often eat lunch right at my drawing board. When I agree to do a book I work out a schedule with the publisher. To finish the art (and sometimes corrections) on time, I must work steadily. I can have more than one project going at a time. If I get stuck on one idea, I work on something else awhile.

3. Where do you work?

Now that I work for myself (including keeping track of money and paying bills), my studio is in my home. I have a large drawing board near large windows, with cabinets and work surfaces on both sides. I keep my marking pens, pencils, paints, and colored papers in all the drawers. On top of the drawers I have jars full of brushes, pens, pencils, scissors, a tape dispenser, a rubber-cement jug, a telephone (I can work while I talk), and a desk calendar to help me keep track of speaking dates at schools and museums. The calendar's usually messy with ink or paint splashes by the end of the week.

4. Do you have any children? Any pets?

I wasn't lucky enough to be a mother, but I try to be a first-rate aunt to my nephew and two nieces. I save pads of paper and colored paper scraps for them to use when they visit. I enjoy seeing their work, and I've been the subject of several of their portraits.

My pets are from all over the world: a wooden porcupine from Santa Fe with broom-bristle quills, about fifty fish and four frogs painted with spots and stripes, an antelope from Africa, a snake my brother made for me, two cloth mice, and a ceramic deer, now in my kitchen.

5. What do you enjoy drawing the most?

I'm especially interested in nature. I use my large library of books to find information about what I draw. If I'm doing a book about birds, I get a stack of books with pictures of woodpeckers, robins, and other birds, so I see where they live and how they eat.

6. Do you ever put people you know in your pictures?

No, I haven't yet. But the cat in *Feathers for Lunch* is my nephew's cat, Bucky. I told Bucky that soon he will be famous!

7. What do you use to make your pictures?

The art technique I use is called collage: cut pieces of paper glued to a backing. Sometimes I paint white paper with watercolors and cut it up, and sometimes I use paper with just one tone. I usually make a dummy with just pencil drawings to show what I want to illustrate on each page. Then I start looking at my subject matter. For *Planting a Rainbow*, I visited flower gardens and parks. I spend a long time checking my facts before I begin to paint. Then I cut out each little piece and glue it on a board until it becomes a bird or a flower. If you look at the Indian corn in *Eating the Alphabet*, you'll see each kernel is a separate piece of paper glued on the page.

Eating the Alphabet: Fruits and Vegetables from A to Z. 1989.
Collage, 8½ × 22″. Published by Harcourt Brace Jovanovich.

8. **How did you get to do your first book?**

A friend in Milwaukee wrote a poem "I Like Orange," which I thought would make a nice book. So I made sketches, a cardboard cover, and a dust jacket, and then sewed the pages together with thread, just as a real book is made. I took it with me on a vacation to New York and saw as many publishers as I could. I was turned down over and over, but the last company bought the book. It's not unusual to be rejected, but if an idea is good, sooner or later it will work out.

Lisa Campbell Ernst

MY STORY

Birthday: March 13, 1957

One of my earliest memories is of drawing one Sunday morning in the preschool room at our church. As I sat working, muffled hymns floated down the hall from the sanctuary where the rest of my family sat. It seems odd now, but I don't remember what I drew. I do remember, though, an incredible feeling of awe, and strength, and magic, in creating a totally new world from a blank piece of paper.

The idea of becoming an artist did not enter my mind. But the idea that I *was* an artist did. In my mind, life was very simple. My older brother was good at tennis. My older sister was good at the piano. And I was the artist of the family.

As I grew older I continued to draw, to create worlds, usually ones made up of animals: our dog, a friend's cat, or the many turtles, snakes, mice, rabbits, lizards, and birds that lived in our Oklahoma neighborhood. Crayons were my medium of choice, and to this day that fresh, waxy smell of a new box can send tingles down my spine.

Books fascinated me. My parents read to me a great deal: A. A. Milne's Winnie-the-Pooh books, the Angus books by Margery Flack (which I'm sure is why I have a Scottish terrier today), the books of H. A. Rey and Dr. Seuss, and big, fat books filled with poetry.

And, as strange as it seems to me now, I also learned about books from a television show called "Captain Kangaroo." The Captain read picture books as part of his show. My first meeting with *Make Way for Ducklings* by Robert McCloskey was through this program. I can still see the sweep of the camera across those ducklings, waddling to follow their mother, and the pure delight I felt.

Another part of the Captain Kangaroo show totally enthralled me as well. It was called the Magic Drawing Board. A squiggle—a messy tangle of a line—was made on the board and then the line was continued, mysteriously, until the squiggle became something recognizable, like a rabbit, or a lady wearing a hat. I thought that was the ultimate challenge for an artist.

My first introduction to the outside art world came in kindergarten. I had drawn a redheaded woodpecker, and my teacher had chosen it for the town's annual school art show. I was thrilled to think of my artwork hanging with all of the big kids' work, and of course had visions of a huge prize ribbon hanging on it come art show day.

When that Sunday finally arrived, my family all climbed into the car and headed downtown to the art center.

As we walked in the door, my eyes quickly searched each art-covered wall. I saw endless drawings of horses and flowers, spaceships and families, on and on, one after another.

And then, rounding a corner, I saw it: my woodpecker—but different. It seems there had been a mix-up. My drawing had been hung sideways. So there, in front of all of Bartlesville, was my wood-pecker, with his beak *not* tapping the side of a tree trunk as I had intended, but instead looking like it had become stuck in the mud. Of course, there was no ribbon. The world was unjust in my eyes at that moment, even though my family all enthusiastically assured me that my bird looked fine just the way it was. I knew better.

But I continued to draw, and there were other years with art shows where my drawings made it to the wall right side up, and even some when I received a ribbon.

As I learned to read and write, my mother made up a game to keep me busy: She would write down a list of things, like "a mouse, a cigar box, a bell, an eraser." And I would be sent off to make up a story using all of those elements. It was great fun. Sometimes, even now, I make up lists for myself.

All through school, I took art lessons, making watercolor paintings and charcoal drawings and clay pots. But *between* all of these "artistic" endeavors was regular life. I rode my bike, had Kool-Aid stands, and played games with the neighborhood kids on hot summer nights. I went on vacations with my family, moved to a new house, baked cakes, collected stamps, and tried—unsuccessfully—to learn to play the piano. And really, all of that played the most important role in making me the artist that I am now. Because those things, those feelings, are what my stories and pictures are about today.

The nice thing is that being an artist now is not so different from being one back in the church preschool room. Now, I have editors, art directors, and deadlines to work with. But when I sit at my table with a blank piece of paper and watch it transform itself into a new world, that feeling—the one of awe, and strength, and magic—is exactly the same. And that, I think, is what becoming an artist is all about.

"Rejoice in who you are! It is your uniqueness that will breathe life into your art."

—Lisa Campbell Ernst

Bluey. Age 7.
Crayon on paper, 11 × 8½".

1. **Where do you get your ideas from?**

Probably everyone marvels at how strange life is: amazing family and friends, odd animals. Happily, my life is full of such characters.

Most ideas begin by seeing something that makes me ask, "Why?" "How?" or "What if . . .?" For example, one hot summer day as I drove down a country road I saw some cows that, as usual, were standing in groups under shade trees—but on this day I got the idea that they were up to something. What? *When Bluebell Sang* was my answer.

2. **What is a normal day like for you?**

I usually work eight to nine hours a day. Before a deadline it can be fourteen to fifteen hours. I love my work, so even a long, tiring day can be exciting. I read the *New York Times* first, then I begin drawing. Early morning's my favorite time to draw. It's quiet and the phone isn't ringing yet.

My drawing board—a giant antique oak one—came from a school in New York. I think about all the students who sat at it long ago, and the artwork they did. I wonder who'll work on it after me, and what kind of art they'll do. If only that board could tell me its stories!

In the afternoon I usually go to the library, or to a great bookstore nearby. I learn a lot looking at all kinds of books, both old and new.

Besides work, I enjoy reading, gardening, fixing up our old house, being with my husband and friends, and playing with my pets.

3. **Where do you work?**

My studio is five minutes away from my house in Kansas City. It's over a music store, so music wafts up through the floor as I work.

4. **Do you have any children? Any pets?**

My husband, Lee, and I don't have children, but we have lots of children friends. We have a dog named Sally who loves going on walks and for rides in the car. When I work at night, Sally comes with me. She likes carrots and broccoli. I also have a gray-and-white rabbit named Penny who lives at my studio. She's great company, and not surprisingly, her favorite treats are carrots and broccoli.

5. What do you enjoy drawing the most?

I've always loved animals, so of course I like to draw them. Even more, I'm intrigued with the bond between animals and humans. It is one of mystery, codependency, and—I hope—respect. I enjoy telling stories about that relationship through words and pictures.

I'm fascinated by our link with the past. Who we are today is a result of those who lived before us. The history of our many cultures, traditions, hopes, and fears interweaves to bring us to the present. That's why many of my stories are set in the past, to celebrate the likenesses and differences between today and yesterday.

6. Do you ever put people you know in your pictures?

I never set out to, but often I draw a character and suddenly realize it looks exactly like a friend or someone in my family. The people around us are what our memory is made up of, so it's only natural that these people show up when we draw from our imagination. It always surprises me, though!

7. What do you use to make your pictures?

The most important thing I use is my imagination—because without that, there can be no magic, or soul, to a drawing.

My materials are pastels, ink, and pencil. Pastels are fine colored chalks I use to color my illustrations. The outline is made with ink in a quill pen. The line shading, or cross-hatching, is made with pencil.

8. How did you get to do your first book?

When I decided to try to illustrate children's books, I was living in New York City. It was a good place to be because so many publishing companies are there. I had no idea how to start and no one to ask for advice. So I put some of my drawings into a portfolio and got out the Yellow Pages. I turned to "Publishers" and called the ones I recognized from my favorite books. I was able to make appointments to show editors and art directors my drawings and was lucky to be offered a book to illustrate from those appointments.

When Bluebell Sang. 1989.
Pastel and ink, 7½ × 10".
Published by Bradbury Press.

MY STORY

Birthday: May 19, 1933

Although I've been drawing since I was four or five years old, my earliest memory of an interest in telling stories with pictures was around the age of nine. Until then, I had mainly copied characters from comic books or from newspaper funnies. I would invent plots, make up stories, and create my own characters for each new story.

I remember my mother helping me in all this by folding many sheets of blank paper in half and then stitching them together, at the fold, on her sewing machine. Then she would tell me to "draw her a book." I would fill up these "mama-made books" from the front cover to the back with my drawings.

I heard about an artist who was teaching at the Police Athletic League (P.A.L.) in my Brooklyn neighborhood and I went right over. There I met Mr. Thipadeaux, who was not only a real live working artist, he was a BLACK ARTIST—the first I had ever met.

I showed him all of my drawings. He immediately discouraged me from copying from comic books. He said, "Tom, drawing from your own imagination is good, but you can also bring something unique to your art by drawing and painting the world right around you—the people and places right in front of you, and the things you see every day. It is important that you see that, and try and show that, too."

With his encouragement I began to create posters for the P.A.L. sports events. I did watercolor sketches from my window, drawings from the P.A.L. window, and my first oil paintings—pictures of my mother and aunt.

These were my first portraits of real people, people close to me. Before that, all of
the comic book characters that I copied or
made up, and even the characters that I saw
in books for adults and children, were all
pictures of white people. Yet this was not
the community or the world I was living in.

Mr. Thipadeaux praised my new work.
He always pushed me to do better and said
he expected much more from me. Some-
times he irritated me by making me draw things over and over. He'd
say, "Tom, you need discipline. Only hard work will develop your skills
so that you can finally put down on paper not just what you see, but
also what you *feel* about the subjects you draw and paint. One day you'll
thank me for pushing you so hard." What I liked most about Mr. Thipadeaux was that he always treated me like an adult and constantly let
me know that he had confidence in me.

Around this time, the art teacher in school gave us a special class
assignment. She assigned a report for Negro History Week on two black
historical figures. I would have to do research at the library. I was more
than familiar with the library's children's room, having spent many days
and hours reading Grimm's fairy tales and books like that, books that
took me to a never-never land, far from Brooklyn, on an imaginary
journey . . . to places that only existed for me in the pages of those books.
But this assignment dealt with real people, two black men out of my
historical past: George Washington Carver, a scientist, and Booker T.
Washington, an educator.

I had to look in a place I had never been—the library adult section.
A librarian directed me to a small room where all the books about
African-Americans were kept. I glided into this wonderful room, packed
full of books on the Black Experience. Here for the first time I read about
people who looked like me. I eagerly read through the material on the
two prominent men and then discovered many more black people from
a past I barely knew existed. Frederick Douglass, Harriet Tubman,
Sojourner Truth, Hannibal . . . on and on.

I read everything my mind could take in, and even though it was difficult, I read some novels like Richard Wright's *Black Boy* and *Native Son*. They left me exhilarated, excited, but also confused; my head was filled with so many unanswered questions. Why had so many of these people gone through so many hardships? Why were we made into slaves, and why were we treated so badly in America?

Would I have to go through these same kinds of things in my life?

When I saw paintings in the few books with art in them by black artists, questions arose in my mind, again. But no one was there to answer them. I looked at those pictures for hours, trying to imagine what each artist had felt . . . I thought I could somehow get answers by staring at the art. The short biographical statements about each artist told me very little about their lives. Had they come out of a community like mine? When did they start drawing and painting the life around them? Did they copy from magazines and books as I did—books that had no images of black people in them at all?

So many questions were left unanswered, until I found the poetry section and the poems of Langston Hughes. His words seemed to light up all those corners of my mind. His word images connected me to that past I was reading about, to the present I was living, and even to the life it turned out that I would experience in the future. For, in his poetry, I could *see* the places and *feel* the faces I was familiar with as clearly as if he had painted them—just for me.

Above all, he showed so much love for his own people and his words spoke directly to that feeling. I yearned to express myself, just like him, with my art. I knew then that one day I wanted to illustrate those books that I had yet to see. I had a constant reminder of that desire every time I thought of Langston's poem "My People."

MY PEOPLE

The night is beautiful, so the faces of my
people. The stars are beautiful, so the eyes
of my people. Beautiful, also, is the sun.
Beautiful, also, are the souls of my people.

BY TOM

madison Square Garden Rodeo (or Circus.)

TOM FEELINGS AGE 6 ?

"Carry a sketchbook wherever you go because it's a record of what you're seeing and feeling."

—Tom Feelings

Madison Square Garden Rodeo (or Circus). Age 6. Pencil, 8 × 10½".

1. Where do you get your ideas from?

I get my ideas from the life around me, by constantly looking at, observing, and taking in all I can see and hear, especially through contact with people—directly and indirectly. I also get ideas by watching films and television and by reading articles and books that interest me. I bring all of this, I believe, to any story I'm going to illustrate.

I read the text of the story thoroughly, looking for visual clues. I jot them down and then select the ideas that best capture what is happening in that part of the story. From these ideas I develop sketches and layouts into final drawings.

2. What is a normal day like for you?

Except for two days a week, when I teach two classes in drawing and illustration, I still wake up at 8:30 every morning. I eat a light breakfast, go directly to my studio, and work until noon. I have a lunch break, then go back to work until about 7 P.M. Then I watch the news of the day on television. I might read some or continue working or listen to music until midnight. Then, I prepare for the next day and finally get in bed around 1 A.M.

3. Where do you work?

I live in a small, two-bedroom house. The front half consists of my living space with a dining room, a kitchen, and so on. The back half of this house is an open loft, a working area. I call this my studio. This is where I do all my painting, drawing, illustrating books, and sometimes sculpture.

4. Do you have any children? Any pets?

I have two sons, aged eighteen and twenty-one. They live in Philadelphia, Pennsylvania, with their mother. She and I have been divorced since 1974.

I have no pets and live alone in South Carolina.

5. What do you enjoy drawing the most?

Primarily people, and all those things related to and affected by human beings.

6. Do you ever put people you know in your pictures?

Yes. In one book I illustrated, *Song of the Empty Bottles*, the main character was a boy about eight years old. He was the same age as my nephew at that time. So I photographed my nephew in different positions and angles. I focused especially on his face and head. I used these photos as reference material so that I would be able to maintain the same likeness of character throughout the book.

I did the same kind of thing with another boy, whom I used as a model for the book *A Quiet Place*.

7. What do you use to make your pictures?

I use different materials. I start with pencil, and sometimes pen and

1. **Where do you get your ideas from?**

    Many different sources. Memories of my childhood show up in *Can I Keep Him?* or *The Mystery of the Missing Red Mitten*. Other ideas come from adult experiences. My rollicking and zany Great Dane pup inspired the Pinkerton series. Still other ideas come from old songs or tales, like *There Was an Old Woman* and *Paul Bunyan*.

    Art is really the language of feeling. It's important to tell about something special to you, to share *your* own story. You can write that story, draw that story, dance that story—whatever form suits you.

2. **What is a normal day like for you?**

    I wake up each morning eager to look at the illustration I worked on the day before. When I'm actually painting and drawing I become so involved that I feel like I am a part of the life of the picture. After a night of separation I am able to judge the work I've done from a more critical point of view, and then I sit down at my drawing table and rework the areas of the illustration that are unsatisfactory. I am in my studio most of the day, and when I'm intensely involved with a project I often work very late into the night. In between work sessions I love to take long walks in the woods with Pinkerton.

3. **Where do you work?**

    I work upstairs on the top floor of the old farmhouse where I've lived for twenty-five years. When my six stepchildren were growing up the house was filled with activity, and I worked in whatever spare corner was available. But they've been off in the world for a number of years now, and I've expanded several small bedrooms into a wonderful studio that has windows overlooking a waterfall and skylights opening into the treetops. There are a number of work nooks, so I can keep several projects under way at the same time, and placed around the room are favorite old toys and pictures that I've collected.

4. **Do you have any children? Any pets?**

    I've raised six stepchildren who are all grown up, and now I have seven grandchildren. Most of my books are dedicated to my family.

We've had numerous dogs and cats over the years, including Pinkerton and Rose, who appear in my books.

5.   What do you enjoy drawing the most?

I love to draw almost anything, but I enjoy animals the most. I usually manage to have animals in the books, even if they're not primary characters. I love drawing trees, architecture—anything.

6.   Do you ever put people you know in your pictures?

Yes, usually my wife, Helen. I've put my children in crowd scenes and even used incidents from their lives that they alone recognize.

7.   What do you use to make your pictures?

I use colored inks, watercolors, acrylic paints, and various types of pencils, trying to pick whichever one will best express the feeling or mood I want for a particular illustration. I work somewhat intensely, and I like to surround myself with my materials so that the momentum doesn't have to be interrupted by a search through cupboards and drawers when I suddenly need a certain color, pencil, or brush.

8.   How did you get to do your first book?

I'd always been interested in doing books, but I was interested in many kinds of artwork at the same time. I wrote a story called "The Orchard Rat" and sent it to a publisher. On the basis of the sketches I sent with it, they asked me to illustrate a number of books. After much rewriting, the original story was published as *The Orchard Cat*.

Best Friends. 1986.
Colored inks, acrylics, and watercolor, 8¼ × 9".
Published by Dial Books for Young Readers.

MY STORY

Birthday: December 22, 1939

I think I might have first gotten interested in art because of my two older brothers who drew. They liked to make pictures of airplanes, cars, things of that sort. I got started by mimicking them, trying to draw what they drew.

I remember an incident in the first grade when I was growing up in Philadelphia that sort of shaped the idea in my mind that I wanted to be an artist. For a Fire Prevention Week project I got to draw a red fire engine on a big sheet of brown paper. I got a lot of attention from that and I liked it. I was encouraged by my teacher and, as I kept drawing, I became the "class artist."

Probably part of the reason that I focused on my drawing so much was that I felt I wasn't very strong in other areas. I was able to escape some projects by drawing the assignments.

I was able to take private art classes when I was in junior high school. My father was a handyman who did painting, plumbing, electrical work, gardening—a bit of everything. He had several clients who knew of private art classes and I remember taking classes in different neighborhoods. Usually they were still-life painting classes.

When I was eleven or twelve years old I had a newspaper stand on the corner of a fairly large intersection in Philadelphia. I would take my drawing pad and sketch while I was there. An artist named John Liney, who was a cartoonist for the Henry comics, noticed me drawing. He took me to visit his studio, which was about a block away. From time to time I would go to see him and he would give me different materials to work with, different art supplies. So at that early age I had a sense that it was possible to make a living doing art. Knowing him and seeing how he worked helped me understand the possibilities of using one's talents.

One early influence was the work of Arthur Rackham, who was an illustrator of children's stories. I liked the quality of his drawing and how he used color.

I later went to Dobbins Vocational High School and took commercial art classes that introduced me to lettering and technical drawing, airbrush, and all kinds of media. In the twelfth grade, we even attended some figure-drawing evening classes.

There was a competition for scholarships to the Philadelphia Museum College of Art. Only four or five were available. I had to show a portfolio and write a paper stating why I wanted to attend. It felt great to win a scholarship, and I began studying advertising and design. But I soon realized that I enjoyed painting and printmaking classes even more, and drawing became very important to me.

I began doing greeting cards, advertising, and textbook illustration in Boston. The textbook work made me realize I liked illustration that was tied to a story.

Book illustration seemed freer than some of the work I was doing. Working with a manuscript was very exciting. I also began to put some effort into looking at and researching African-American artists. I admired Charles White, whose strong, graphic drawings gave such dignity to the black figure. I was also impressed by the photographs of James Van Der Zee. If you look at the work of these two men, I think you'll see their influence in my book *Home Place*.

I've won a lot of awards for my art and it feels wonderful to know that my work is appreciated. My work includes a mixture of things that I, myself, have appreciated. In some ways, it is a testimony to be able to state through my art, "Yes, these people have influenced me, and I'd like to say it now."

"Draw as much as possible if you want to one day be an illustrator. Especially, draw from life."

—Jerry Pinkney

Boy with a Wagon. Age 7. Watercolor, 12 × 9".

1. Where do you get your ideas from?

Most of my work comes from the text, which I use as a sort of springboard. I try to find stories that allow me to make some kind of personal statement. For example, I'll find manuscripts that deal with the African-Americans and our history in this country. So the ideas come from the story but also from my own personal commitment.

2. What is a normal day like for you?

Part of the year I teach for two days a week at the University of Delaware. Those days start early and end very late. When I'm working in the studio I'm at the drawing board between eight-thirty and nine o'clock in the morning. I get started easily and work straight through the day, taking a break for lunch or maybe to take a walk. Usually, my day ends between eight-thirty and ten o'clock at night. So many things that can happen during the day need to be taken care of as well. I might spend a lot of time on the phone discussing work, or packing up art that must be shipped to a gallery or publisher, running out to get Xerox copies of things. All of this accounts for a fairly long day.

3. Where do you work?

I work in my studio right in the house. I have a screened-in porch that looks out into the woods. So it's really quite a nice environment with good space and lots of light.

4. Do you have any children? Any pets?

Yes, I have four children. Troy Bernadette Johnson is the director of Child Life at Jacobi Hospital and mother of our granddaughter, Gloria, who appears on the cover and inside of the book *Pretend You're a Cat*.

Brian Pinkney is an illustrator, and a very active one in the area of children's books.

Scott Cannon Pinkney is an art director at a large advertising agency. He's married and living in England for a year.

And our son Myles Carter Pinkney is a childcare worker at the Anderson School. He's studying photography. Myles and his wife, Sandra, have two children.

5. What do you enjoy drawing the most?

It varies. Perhaps I most enjoy drawing animals. Next to that would be using animals in an anthropomorphic way—giving them human characteristics, like dressing them in clothes or giving them human expressions. Combining them with people fascinates me and gives me so many areas to work on that I enjoy.

I try to keep a balance in my work. If I find that I'm working on projects that include an awful lot of animals and less people I want to balance it, so I go back and forth. When I get to a point where I've had it with drawing animals, I'll pick a project where there are more human figures involved. The variety can be quite, quite exciting.

I've always tried to focus on the things that give me the most enjoyment. Part of me always needs to try to do something that I've never done before or to bring a different point of view to my work. Often, this involves working on things that make me uncomfortable at the time. But the idea is to move through that uncomfortable stage and learn how to resolve the problem I'm having in my work and face it head on. Hopefully, that helps bring a freshness to the work.

For instance, for a while I showed most of the figures and animals in my paintings from a close-up point of view. There's not very much depth in those compositions, usually. Now I'm doing just the opposite of that and moving back and seeing characters in a much larger setting. That keeps me interested in what I'm doing. I like variety.

6. Do you ever put people you know in your pictures?

Yes—especially my family. When my children were very young they were always turning up in my work. I think Brian has been a major character in a book and Myles and Scott and Troy have been on covers. Gloria, my wife, models for me all the time and also helps take photographs of the models.

Very often, when I get a manuscript I have to find models for the characters in the story. They're people that I don't know or don't know very well and, with the way I work, I like to introduce the models to the text and often have them act it out. Before it's all over, I end up knowing them very, very well because we've shared this kind of experience.

7. What do you use to make your pictures?

My work is done in pencil and watercolor on paper, usually. But I tend to use a lot of different media along with the watercolor: pastel, color pencils, and Cray-Pas. My worktable is just full of all these materials, and I use whatever I think will help me in getting the kind of effect that I want for the pictures.

8. How did you get to do your first book?

My first book, *The Adventures of Spider* by Joyce Arkhurst, was published by Little, Brown in 1964. The book came as a result of my being in the Boston area where there are certainly a lot of book publishers. I had gotten some very nice recognition from art shows in which my work had appeared.

I think that it also had a lot to do with the climate of the times. There were publishers who were interested in publishing African-American writers. I think there was an awareness, if not pressure, that the African-American artist could perhaps bring something unique to a text, something more personal. The publishers were actually looking for someone black to do this particular project, which was a collection of West African folktales. I showed them my portfolio, they liked my work, and that's how I got to do my first book.

Home Place by Crescent Dragonwagon. 1990.
Watercolor, 7 × 9½″. Published by Macmillan Publishing Company.

Amy Schwartz

MY STORY

Birthday: April 2, 1954

I can't say there was one moment when I decided to be an artist, because there was never a time when I didn't want to be one. I was always drawing when I was a child. In school I was constantly getting in trouble for doodling during math, music, and social studies.

I also drew pictures at home after school. Sometimes I would set up still lifes; more often I would work from my imagination. And other times I would get together with my friend Wendy, and we would draw together. We would take turns selecting the subject matter, each of us choosing, of course, themes at which we considered ourselves expert.

My family encouraged my interest in art. My mother also does artwork, and I remember watching her sketch. She worked in pencil, pastels, and watercolor. Sometimes she would draw from life, using the family as models. On vacations she often traveled with a sketchbook, recording landscapes and the local people. I loved it when she would let me use her creamy oil pastels.

My parents also took me with them to museums and art shows. They enrolled me in art classes at the zoo and the fine arts museum. For my birthdays, I often received art supplies as presents. That's how I got my first oil paints, small canvas boards, acrylic paints in tubes, and the accompanying long, stiff brushes—all very professional, I thought.

Being an artist gave me an identity at school and within my family. It was important to me to have a talent I was recognized for. I was a quiet, daydreamy child, and so I found drawing—a private, reflective activity —very appealing.

For birthdays and every year at Hanuk-kah, I made cards for my sisters, parents, and grandmother. I usually painted some sort of portrait of the person receiving the card—my father playing tennis, my sister Becky lighting the menorah, and so forth. This was my favorite form of art making: painting small, personal pictures that would please someone I was close to, perhaps make them laugh. Making picture books gives me a similar kind of satisfaction today.

I loved to read when I was a child. If I liked a book, I would often start it over from the beginning as soon as I finished. I preferred long books, wanting to live in the story's fantasy as long as I could. I learned my love of reading from my parents, both of whom are always reading. My mother helped me choose books at the library, sometimes from the mysterious adult section. I also selected books on my own. At a certain age I concentrated on books by authors whose last names began with W, Y, and Z. I had the mistaken notion that the volumes at that far end of the children's book section were the most advanced.

I also loved looking at a book's illustrations. When I was small I accepted the illustrations as being true to life, however fantastic or styl-ized they might have been. As I got a little older, I also became aware that these pictures were pieces of art, that they were made by an artist, with materials on paper, and were to be admired as such. I think this is where my desire to illustrate books began.

"Art improves with practice. A loving familiarity with books and stories will help you think like an illustrator."

—Amy Schwartz

Rainstorm. Age 10. Tempera, 18 × 12″.

1. Where do you get your ideas from?

My stories always begin with something real from my life. My first story, *Begin at the Beginning*, is a combination of autobiography and fiction. I had enrolled in a children's book writing and illustration class and was making my first attempts at writing a story. I sat down to work, and sat there, and sat there. I sharpened all my pencils. I got up and drank a glass of water. Then I went and looked in the mirror for a while, and so forth.

Finally, I started writing out a diary entry about how I was feeling and why I thought it was so hard to get started. I also made a list of all the ridiculous things I was doing to avoid writing. This diary entry eventually became *Begin at the Beginning*, the story of a little girl and her difficulties getting started on a creative project.

The story *Oma and Bobo* is based on real characters. Oma was my grandmother, and Bobo was our family dog when I was growing up. The book is about the relationship between Oma and Bobo, which changes from one of animosity to one of great affection. That relationship was very real, as are the personalities of Oma and Bobo.

Bobo's dog training class and final dog show are also real. Unfor-

derful Flight to the Mushroom Planet. I loved the story and the art. To this day, whenever I smell hard-boiled eggs I think of how Chuck and David saved the planet with the sulfur-smelling eggs.

From then on I drew only "space stuff."

See . . .

THE OTHER STAGES

Over the years I went through a lot of other stages, too—the CAR AND SUBMARINE STAGE, the BASEBALL STAGE, the SUPERHERO STAGE, the BUG STAGE, and so on.

And each stage had its moments. When I was ten, I made an animated flip-book of a baseball player pitching. When I was fourteen, I sent samples of my superheroes to Marvel Comics and they actually answered back with a letter of encouragement and a free sheet of the official art board that their artists used (Wow! Free paper!).

For a while I was into trees. By the way, have you ever noticed that all trees drawn by kids must have this thing on them?

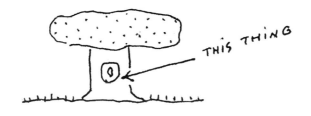

We don't know what makes us draw it, or even what it is, for that matter—it's just something we're born with.

In junior high and high school I received a lot of encouragement from my art teachers. My junior high teacher, Ms. Ng, entered some of my work in an art show and it actually won!!!*

Then in high school, Mr. Baughman convinced me to experiment with different types of materials. I tried acrylics, oil paints, pen and ink, and watercolor. I learned that different media could create different moods (watercolors make great sad-rainy-day pictures).

Mr. Baughman also exposed me to all kinds of art and illustration in books. When I finally did my own book, *Flying Jake*, I dedicated it to him.

I am glad things worked out the way they did and I am able to spend my life drawing pictures for a living. I can't imagine what would've happened if I had decided to become a mathematician.

*"Honorable Mention"

"*To be an artist you have to keep on doing art— just draw, draw, draw!*"

—Lane Smith

Mr. Space. Age 8. Pencil and crayon, 5 × 2¾".

1. **Where do you get your ideas from?**

I get my ideas from everything! Like the way somebody parts their hair might give me an idea for a picture of a winding river, or shoestrings in knots can inspire drawings of futuristic highways. Of course if that doesn't work, I just copy the drawings from my comic books.

2. **What is a normal day like for you?**

A normal day for me is probably a lot like a day for you. I wake up and watch cartoons while eating my cereal. I walk downstairs to my work area and start to draw and paint.

Most of my work is for magazines, so I had to learn to work fast. For example, I might get a call on Monday for a drawing that they need by Wednesday! They send me the story, I read it, then start thinking up ideas—and if that doesn't work I just copy the drawings from my comic books.

Around lunchtime I take a walk, watch more cartoons, eat a sandwich, walk some more, more cartoons, go back to work, then . . .

I like to watch cartoons.

3. **Where do you work?**

I work in my apartment.

I have a little studio downstairs.

Like a lot of New Yorkers, I have a great view. It is of a brick wall. Once, after looking at that brick wall every day for three years, I got curious. I wanted to see what was on the other side of it.

I went exploring.

I walked out my door, around the corner, and over a fence to where the wall was. I tried to go around it but couldn't. There were more brick walls blocking my way. It was dark. I fumbled in that shadowy place looking for a secret passage that would lead me to the other side. Looking behind my back, I could see my little studio (my window needed washing).

Then, my fingers felt a doorknob! I looked up. In faded letters, the door was marked Entrance. I cautiously pressed against it. It creaked the kind of creak that you hear on those "Halloween sound effects" records.

I stuck my head in, then the rest of me. I was on the other side!

And there, behind the brick wall were . . . a couple of smelly trash cans and some empty boxes. Bummer.

I went home.

I cleaned my window.

I looked around at all my stuff. For inspiration, I've surrounded myself with things that I liked when I was a kid—Viewmasters, books, toys, puppets, flip-books, games, and so on.

They helped me to think.

I started to draw.

I drew some weird purple-haired monsters and a couple of green castles.

4. **Do you have any children? Any pets?**

Yes, I have one child. His name is A.J. He is a cat. He is fat.

5. **What do you enjoy drawing the most?**

Faces.

6. **Do you ever put people you know in your pictures?**

Not directly, but elements of them creep into my work, and that big, fat cat in *The Big Pets* looks very familiar.

7. **What do you use to make your pictures?**

Oil paints, and sometimes I add (collage) real things into my illustrations like sticks, old photos, newspaper clippings, and so on.

I did a book with Jon Scieszka called *The True Story of the Three Little Pigs!* I collaged a bunch of stuff into that one. Jon said, "How creative!" Little did he know it was really saving me a lot of painting time.

Heh, heh.

8. **How did you get to do your first book?**

I got to do my first book in a backward kind of way.

Traditionally, the story comes first, then the illustrator is hired to draw the pictures. In my case, I did almost all of the paintings first. I just did them, I didn't even know exactly what to do with them. I thought that they might make a nice Halloween book, so I took them to Macmillan Publishing and then they found a writer to do the words.

I was very lucky because the writer they got was Eve Merriam. After that I was hooked. Now I am writing and illustrating my own books.

The Big Pets. 1991.
Oil painting, 12½ × 9″. Published by Viking Penguin.

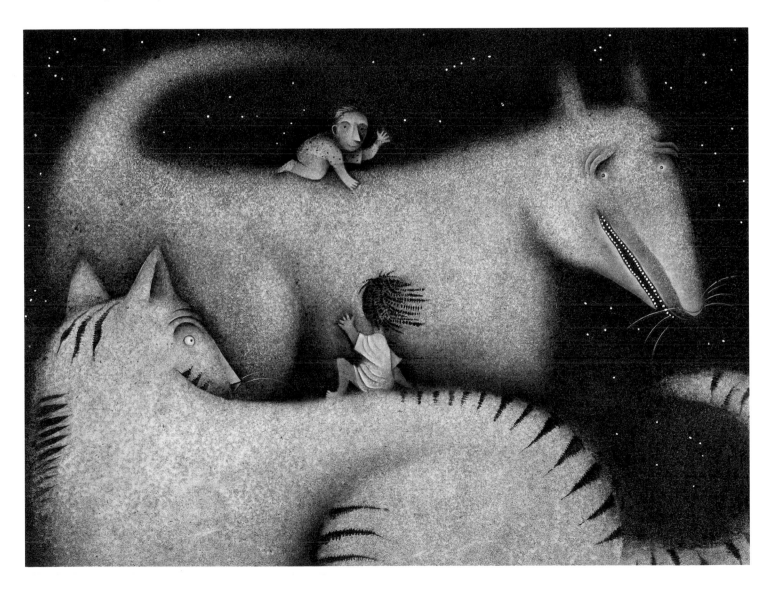

C. [signature]

MY STORY

Birthday: June 18, 1949

I didn't take art classes in high school and didn't decide that art was my calling until I got into college. The thing that made me decide that it was what I wanted to do was probably just the pleasure that I got out of it. I realized that as an adult I could have the same fun I had as a kid making art. And to be able to get a college degree for it was really a surprise to me.

When I was a kid I was a pretty good artist. I could draw cartoon characters very well, which is, I think, a sort of common sign of early artistic ability. I particularly liked to draw Dagwood Bumstead, who wasn't really that popular a character, either. It wasn't the sort of thing that would impress your friends. But I thought I drew him pretty well.

I always looked forward to art class. We had an art teacher who came to give us lessons twice a week in my school, but I never took outside lessons.

I actually chose to go to art school because, at the time, I thought it would be an easy way for me to earn a college degree. So it was a decision I made partly because of the pleasure that I got from art but also because I thought it would be somewhat easy.

I thought that studying art in college might mean that I would be taking one or two art classes a week along with all the regular classes.

I had no clear idea of what it meant to be an art student or, for that matter, an artist.

When I got to art school I discovered it was much more intense than

8. **How did you get to do your first book?**

I'd been drawing pictures, almost as a hobby. I'd spend the day making sculpture and then when I came home I'd spend some time doing these little drawings. A friend of mine thought that the drawings seemed to have a narrative quality . . . they seemed to tell a story. This friend suggested that I should try to find an opportunity to use my drawing skills as an illustrator. He thought that book illustration was a high calling, partly because he was a book illustrator. So I did some drawings and I worked out a little bit of a story and I showed it to some publishers and they all liked it. So I just signed a contract and finished the book.

The Stranger. 1986.
Watercolor, 14 × 11″. Published by Houghton Mifflin.

David Wiesner

MY STORY

Birthday: February 5, 1956

I think that I always knew I wanted to become an artist. I can't remember a time when I wasn't drawing and painting pictures.

My oldest sister and my brother were artistic, and watching them draw fascinated me. They had many different art supplies around the house. There was, and still is, something very appealing about art materials: Boxes of pastels, with incredibly colored, thin, square sticks, fitting snugly into the slots in their trays. Little ink bottles with rubber stoppers and pens with interchangeable metal tips. The look, smell, and feel of rich black ink going onto bright white paper in broad, flat strokes or thin, sharp lines. I found this captivating.

In our town, the housepaint and wallpaper store also sold art supplies. I loved looking at all the exotic things they had for sale. Sandpaper blocks to sharpen pencils. Rows of numbered pencils, and erasers that could be pulled like taffy. Thin drawers full of tubes of paint that seemed so much more grown up than the kind we used at school. Complicated easels and wooden boxes to hold everything.

My parents and friends soon saw that I had more than a passing interest in art. It came to define much of my image. Relatives gave me art-related birthday gifts. At school I became "the kid who could draw," a unique distinction, like "brainiest" or "best athlete"—but somehow different. A little weird, actually. I like that.

In my kindergarten class, we had an "art corner." There was an easel with a large pad of paper and poster paints. One day I was painting a picture of a red house. I can vividly recall my intense frustration because this picture just didn't look like I wanted it to.

As I got a little older, I began copying pictures: cartoons, comic books, and magazine illustrations. But mostly dinosaurs. I loved them. The *World Book Encyclopedia* published a book about the history of the earth, full of very realistic dinosaur pictures that I drew over and over again. They were in black and white and had a hazy quality to them (bad printing, I think). For a long time, even after I should have known better, I thought they were photographs of dinosaurs.

I found out a few years ago that these particular paintings are murals in the Chicago Field Museum. I've since seen them in person. They were painted by Charles Knight, the first and most famous painter of dinosaurs. They are still impressive, and they are in color!

I'm the youngest of five children. As I said, my oldest sister and my brother (who also played many musical instruments) had artistic talent; another sister went on to study as an operatic soprano. So my parents were prepared for my interests. They always encouraged me, never pushing me to do something more conventional. Maybe because of that support, I never had to take a stand and say, "I'm going to be an artist, no matter what anybody says." It was the natural thing to do.

Early on Saturday, after the agricultural shows, was a TV program called "You Are an Artist" with Jon Gnagy. He'd do pastel or charcoal drawings of a still life, a landscape, or a portrait on his easel. I was amazed at how easily he made marks and created pictures. And he was cool: mustache, beard, flannel shirts with sleeves rolled up to the elbows. Now *this* guy was an artist. I had all his instruction books.

My third-grade class wrote essays on what we wanted to be when we grew up. To me it was obvious. We read them aloud, and I told about the types of paintings I would some day try. I'd have turtles with paintbrushes tied to their backs walking around on a big sheet of paper (I got chuckles from the class and the teacher). Or I'd fill squirt guns with different colored paints and shoot at the canvas. I actually tried this with friends! Well, it *sounded* like a good idea.

One of the only discouraging childhood experiences about my artwork happened in the fourth grade. During study time I was drawing a picture. My teacher took it away and wrote an angry note home to my mother. "David would rather be drawing pictures than doing his work!!!" I couldn't believe it, *three* exclamation points. We didn't get along well for the rest of the year. School "art classes" were pretty uninspiring. I did my best work on textbook covers I made. Art never seemed to be taken as seriously as other subjects.

In the eighth grade, a big career day was held. Months before, we wrote suggestions for careers we wanted to hear about. On the big day, guest speakers from many fields came to talk. We each chose two sessions to attend, but there wasn't one that came close to an art-related field. I saw some guy talk about oceanography.

In high school it actually sank in that I was going to be an artist. My friends read catalogs and saw guidance counselors to pick what they'd study in college. I felt something was wrong. I already knew. I'd always known. I half expected to hear, "No, put away those paints and choose a *real* career." My parents were excited about my choice, too. As I looked into art schools, I felt like doors were being thrown wide open. Until then my art was a private thing, but at art school I found a place where everyone was "the kid who could draw."

"Drawing is the basic tool for all art. So draw as much as possible because the more you draw, the better you get."

—David Wiesner

Red House. Age 5. Poster paint, 24 × 18″.

1.   **Where do you get your ideas from?**

I get ideas from many different places, often while thinking about an object or animal or place. I try to picture the thing in a new way or I see it doing something impossible. I might think "What if . . . ?" I painted a cover for an issue of *Cricket* magazine that had lots of frog stories in it. As I sketched I thought, "What if frogs could fly?" I had drawn a frog on a lily pad, and suddenly saw the lily pad as a flying carpet! The picture became a dozen frogs on lily pads, flying out of a swamp.

2.   **What is a normal day like for you?**

Usually, after breakfast, I'm at my drawing table working on my latest book. I might take the subway into New York City to see my editor or art director about the book. I may get art supplies or go to the library to find reference pictures for a painting. One branch of the New York Public Library has a large room filled with rows and rows of filed pictures of animals, plants, cars, costumes, and much more. If I have to draw an aardvark, or clothes someone wore in fifteenth-century France, I can usually find pictures of these things there.

3.   **Where do you work?**

I live with my wife, Kim, in Brooklyn, New York. Our apartment building used to be a factory. Kim is a surgeon and goes to work at a hospital each day. The studio where I do my artwork is in our home, so I only have to travel across the apartment to get to work.

4.   **Do you have any children? Any pets?**

No, we don't. So I work alone all day, listening to music as I work.

5.   **What do you enjoy drawing the most?**

The "What if . . . ?" situations I described are what I enjoy the most. I've also developed a tendency to put fish in many of my books and pictures. They are interesting to draw, so I try to have a fish turn up in each book. Sometimes I draw an actual fish. Other times, it is a design on cloth or carved into a piece of furniture.

6. **Do you ever put people you know in your pictures?**

I almost always use a person I know as the model for each character in my books, although it may not look like that person when I finish. Many of my friends, my wife, and my family have been models. Recently I was painting a picture of an old wizard and used myself as the model. My wife took photographs of me in the positions the wizard would be in. Since I'm not an old man, I added long gray hair, wrinkles, and an old robe to make me look like an old wizard.

7. **What do you use to make your pictures?**

If I work in black and white, I usually use pencil or charcoal.

Mostly I work in watercolor. I'll soak watercolor paper in the bath-

tub for ten minutes, then tape it to a thin flat board. As it dries, it gets taut, like a drum, and won't get lumpy if I put wet paint on it.

8. How did you get to do your first book?

My first book, *Honest Andrew*, was about a family of otters. I did it a year after I finished art school. During that year, I'd shown many publishers my artwork, hoping I would get to do a book for them. Finally, an editor, Barbara Lucas, asked me to read a story she had and to draw a scene from it so she could see how my characters would look. She liked it very much and decided that I should illustrate *Honest Andrew*. That picture is still one of my favorite paintings.

Tuesday. 1991.
Watercolor, 20 × 8″. Published by Clarion Books.

GLOSSARY

acrylics Plasticlike paints that stick to almost any surface, dry fast, and then aren't affected by water. Light colors can be painted over dried, dark colors.

agent A person who shows your work to clients to find work for you.

airbrush A small spray gun that blows out colored ink in a smooth, continuous tone as a spray paint can does, but the area covered can be controlled.

art director A person in publishing or advertising who works with artists and editors on the design, picks the lettering used, and gets the art printed right.

caricature A cartoon drawing of a person that usually exaggerates some special feature that they have, such as bushy eyebrows or big ears.

charcoal A dark or black stick made from animal or vegetable material (like wood that has been charred) that can be used for drawing. Because it can be very powdery, it smears very well.

collage An artistic composition made by gluing different materials, such as paper, photographs, cloth, and so on, onto a surface.

cross-hatching A drawing technique that uses lots of little lines crossing back and forth to color in an area.

deadline The date a job must be finished.

drafting Making technical drawings, designs, or sketches, usually with tools like rulers, compasses, and technical pens.

editor Many children's book editors choose the story, find an illustrator, and help the author and artist bring words and pictures together into a finished book.

dummy A handmade model of a book that shows sketches of what will take place on each page and also indicates where the words will appear.

fantasy A story, a picture, or a thought created in your imagination.

gouache Watercolor with white added (except for black gouache). It dries lighter than it looks when wet and can dry in a very even, flat color.

landscapes Scenes of outdoor settings: trees, mountains, lakes, and so on.

layout A plan that shows where type and art will fit on a page.

matting Making a border out of a piece of cardboard, called *matt board*, to frame a picture.

medium The kind of art material that is used in any picture. Plural: *media.*

oil paint Paint that is made from mixing powdered colors with oil. Oil paints take a longer time to dry than most other paints.

pastels Colored chalks that are pressed into sticks, made into pencils, or come as crayon-like sticks called **oil pastels**. Both types of pastels come in intense colors and work best on rough paper. Regular pastels can be smudged to blend together but it is hard to put one color right on top of another—they won't mix easily. The colors can be very strong. They work best on rough paper and smear very easily. The oil pastels can be mixed on top of each other, but because they are oily, they smudge more easily than they smear.

portfolio A collection of samples of an artist's work, usually put into a carrying case to show to possible clients.

publisher The person or company that produces books, magazines, or news-papers. People in a book publishing company see to it that stories get illustrated, printed, and sent as books to libraries, stores, and schools.

sculpture Three-dimensional art made from any of a wide variety of materials such as wood, metal, or stone.

stained glass Colored-glass pieces used in making windows. Differently colored pieces can be put together to form a picture or a pattern.

still life A picture showing mostly nonliving objects, often objects put together by the artist just for the purpose of painting or drawing them.

tempera A strong paint, such as poster paint, that contains some oil but mixes with water and dries very fast. *Egg tempera* is actually mixed with egg yolk. If used too thickly, the paint can crack when it has dried.

watercolor In pans, tubes, or bottles, these colors are finely ground-up pigments, some natural and some chemical, that are mixed with water.

woodcut An image is drawn on a woodblock, and the wood is cut away with special knives until only the lines of the drawing are still standing. Ink is rolled over the lines, and the wood is pressed onto paper to print the picture.

BOOKS BY THE ARTISTS

All of the artists were asked to name five favorite books that they've illustrated. If the artist didn't also write the book, the author's name is given so you'll be able to find it in your library or bookstore.

VICTORIA CHESS
Alfred's Alphabet Walk. New York: Greenwillow Books, 1979.

A Hippopotomusn't by J. Patrick Lewis. Illustrated by Victoria Chess. New York: Dial Books for Young Readers, 1990.

Poor Esmé. New York: Holiday House, 1982.

Tales for the Perfect Child by Florence Parry Heide. Illustrated by Victoria Chess. New York: Lothrop, Lee & Shepard, 1985.

Three Blind Mice by John W. Ivimey. Illustrated by Victoria Chess. New York: Dial Books for Young Readers, 1990.

PAT CUMMINGS
Clean Your Room, Harvey Moon! New York: Bradbury Press, 1991.

C.L.O.U.D.S. New York: Lothrop, Lee & Shepard, 1986.

Jimmy Lee Did It. New York: Lothrop, Lee & Shepard, 1985.

Just Us Women by Jeannette Caines. Illustrated by Pat Cummings. New York: Harper & Row, 1982.

Storm in the Night by Mary Stolz. Illustrated by Pat Cummings. New York: Harper & Row, 1988.

LEO AND DIANE DILLON
Aida by Leontyne Price. Illustrated by Leo and Diane Dillon. San Diego: Harcourt Brace Jovanovich, 1990.

Brother to the Wind by Mildred Pitts Walter. Illustrated by Leo and Diane Dillon. New York: Lothrop Lee & Shepard, 1985.

The Porcelain Cat by Michael Hearn. Illustrated by Leo and Diane Dillon. Boston: Little, Brown, 1987.

The Tale of the Mandarin Ducks by Katherine Paterson. Illustrated by Leo and Diane Dillon. New York: Lodestar Books, 1990.

Why Mosquitoes Buzz in People's Ears by Verna Aardema. Illustrated by Leo and Diane Dillon. New York: Dial Books for Young Readers, 1975.

RICHARD EGIELSKI
Hey, Al by Arthur Yorinks. Illustrated by Richard Egielski. New York: Farrar, Straus & Giroux, 1986.

Louis the Fish by Arthur Yorinks. Illustrated by Richard Egielski. New York: Farrar, Straus & Giroux, 1980.

Oh, Brother by Arthur Yorinks. Illustrated by Richard Egielski. New York: Farrar, Straus & Giroux, 1989.

The Little Father by Gelett Burgess. Illustrated by Richard Egielski. New York: Farrar, Straus & Giroux, 1985.

The Tub People by Pam Conrad. Illustrated by Richard Egielski. New York: Harper & Row, 1989.

LOIS EHLERT

Color Farm. Philadelphia: J. B. Lippincott, 1990.

Color Zoo. Philadelphia: J. B. Lippincott, 1989.

Eating the Alphabet: Fruits and Vegetables from A–Z. San Diego: Harcourt Brace Jovanovich, 1989.

Feathers for Lunch. San Diego: Harcourt Brace Jovanovich, 1990.

Fish Eyes. San Diego: Harcourt Brace Jovanovich, 1990.

LISA CAMPBELL ERNST

Ginger Jumps. New York: Bradbury Press, 1990.

Miss Penny and Mr. Grubbs. New York: Bradbury Press, 1991.

Nattie Parsons' Good Luck Lamb. New York: Viking Penguin, 1988.

Sam Johnson and the Blue Ribbon Quilt. New York: Lothrop, Lee & Shepard, 1983.

When Bluebell Sang. New York: Bradbury Press, 1989.

TOM FEELINGS

Black Pilgrimage. New York: Lothrop, Lee & Shepard, 1972.

Daydreamers by Eloise Greenfield. Illustrated by Tom Feelings. New York: Dial Books for Young Readers, 1981.

Jambo Means Hello: Swahili Alphabet Book by Muriel Feelings. Illustrated by Tom Feelings. New York: Dial Books for Young Readers, 1974.

Moja Means One: A Swahili Counting Book by Muriel Feelings. Illustrated by Tom Feelings. New York: Dial Books for Young Readers, 1971.

Now Sheba Sings the Song by Maya Angelou. Illustrated by Tom Feelings. New York: Dial Books for Young Readers, 1987.

STEVEN KELLOGG

Best Friends. New York: Dial Books for Young Readers, 1986.

Engelbert the Elephant by Tom Paxton. Illustrated by Steven Kellogg. New York: Morrow Junior Books, 1990.

Jack and the Beanstalk. New York: Morrow Junior Books, 1991.

Pecos Bill. New York: Morrow Junior Books, 1986.

A Rose For Pinkerton. New York: Dial Books for Young Readers, 1981.

JERRY PINKNEY

Further Tales of Uncle Remus by Julius Lester. Illustrated by Jerry Pinkney. New York: Dial Books for Young Readers, 1989.

Mirandy and Brother Wind by Patricia C. McKissack. Illustrated by Jerry Pinkney. New York: Alfred A. Knopf, 1988.

The Patchwork Quilt by Valerie Flournoy. Illustrated by Jerry Pinkney. New York: Dial Books for Young Readers, 1985.

The Talking Eggs by Robert D. San Souci. Illustrated by Jerry Pinkney. New York: Dial Books for Young Readers, 1989.

Turtle in July by Marilyn Singer. Illustrated by Jerry Pinkney. New York: Macmillan Publishing Company, 1989.

AMY SCHWARTZ

Annabelle Swift, Kindergartner. New York: Orchard Books, 1988.

Bea and Mr. Jones. New York: Bradbury Press, 1982.

Camper of the Week. New York: Orchard Books, 1991.

How I Captured a Dinosaur by Henry Schwartz. Illustrated by Amy Schwartz. New York: Orchard Books, 1989.

Mother Goose's Little Misfortunes by Leonard S. Marcus and Amy Schwartz. Illustrated by Amy Schwartz. New York: Bradbury Press, 1990.

LANE SMITH

The Big Pets. New York: Viking, 1991.

Flying Jake. New York: Macmillan Publishing Company, 1988.

Glasses *Who Needs 'Em.* New York: Viking Penguin, 1991.

Halloween ABC by Eve Merriam. Illustrated by Lane Smith. New York: Macmillan Publishing Company, 1987.

The True Story of the Three Little Pigs! by Jon Scieszka. Illustrated by Lane Smith. New York: Viking Penguin, 1989.

CHRIS VAN ALLSBURG

Jumanji. Boston: Houghton Mifflin Company, 1981.

The Mysteries of Harris Burdick. Boston: Houghton Mifflin Company, 1984.

Two Bad Ants. Boston: Houghton Mifflin Company, 1988.

The Wreck of the Zephyr. Boston: Houghton Mifflin Company, 1982.

The Z Was Zapped. Boston: Houghton Mifflin Company, 1988.

DAVID WIESNER

Free Fall. New York: Lothrop, Lee & Shepard, 1988.

Hurricane. New York: Clarion Books, 1990.

The Loathsome Dragon by Kim Kahng and David Wiesner. Illustrated by David Wiesner. New York: Putnam, 1987.

The Sorcerer's Apprentice by Marianna Mayer. Illustrated by David Wiesner. New York: Bantam, 1989.

ACKNOWLEDGMENTS

Grateful acknowledgment is given to the artists who participated in this book, for permission to reproduce their photographs and samples of their childhood artwork. Our appreciation, too, to the following individuals and publishers.

Page 15. From *A Hippopotomusn't* by J. Patrick Lewis. Pictures by Victoria Chess. Pictures copyright © 1990 by Victoria Chess. Reprinted by permission of the publisher, Dial Books for Young Readers, a division of Penguin USA.

Page 16. Courtesy of Art Cummings.

Page 17. Courtesy of Macmillan/McGraw-Hill School Division.

Page 21. From *C.L.O.U.D.S.* by Pat Cummings. Copyright © 1986 by Pat Cummings. Published by Lothrop, Lee & Shepard Books. Reprinted by permission of William Morrow and Company, Inc.

Pages 28–29. From *The Tale of the Mandarin Ducks* by Katherine Paterson, illustrated by Leo and Diane Dillon. Illustrations copyright © 1990 by Leo and Diane Dillon. Reprinted by permission of the publisher, Lodestar Books, an affiliate of Dutton Children's Books, a division of Penguin USA.

Page 35. Illustration from *Oh, Brother* by Arthur Yorinks, illustrated by Richard Egielski. Illustrations copyright © 1989 by Richard Egielski. Reproduced by permission of Farrar, Straus & Giroux, Inc.

Pages 40–41. "I for Indian Corn" from *Eating the Alphabet: Fruits and Vegetables from A–Z*. Copyright © 1989 by Lois Ehlert, reprinted by permission of Harcourt Brace Jovanovich, Inc.

Page 47. Illustration by Lisa Campbell Ernst. From *When Bluebell Sang* by Lisa Campbell Ernst. Copyright © 1989 by Lisa Campbell Ernst. Reprinted by permission of Bradbury Press, an Affiliate of Macmillan, Inc.

Page 50. "My People." From *Selected Poems* by Langston Hughes. Copyright © 1926 by Alfred A. Knopf, Inc., a subsidiary of Random House, Inc., and renewed 1954 by Langston Hughes. Reprinted by permission of the publisher.

Page 53. Courtesy of Tom Feelings.

Page 59. From *Best Friends* by Steven Kellogg. Copyright © 1986 by Steven Kellogg. Reprinted by permission of the publisher, Dial Books for Young Readers, a division of Penguin USA.

Page 61. Courtesy of Myles Carter Pinkney.

Page 65. Illustration by Jerry Pinkney. From *Home Place* by Crescent Dragonwagon. Illustrations copyright © 1990 by Jerry Pinkney. Reprinted by permission of Macmillan Publishing Company.

Page 71. From *Mother Goose's Little Misfortunes*. Copyright © 1991 by Amy Schwartz. Reprinted by permission of Bradbury Press, an Affiliate of Macmillan, Inc.

Page 77. From *The Big Pets* by Lane Smith. Copyright © 1991 by Lane Smith. Reprinted by permission of the publisher, Viking Penguin, a division of Penguin USA.

Page 83. *The Stranger* by Chris Van Allsburg. Copyright © 1986 by Chris Van Allsburg. Reprinted by permission of Houghton Mifflin Company.

Pages 88–89. *Tuesday* by David Wiesner. Text and illustrations copyright © 1991 by David Wiesner. Reprinted by permission of Clarion Books, a Houghton Mifflin Company imprint.